A Note to Parents and Caregivers:

Read-it! Readers are for children who are just starting on the amazing road to reading. These beautiful books support both the acquisition of reading skills and the love of books.

The RED LEVEL presents familiar topics using common words and repeating sentence patterns.
The BLUE LEVEL presents new ideas using a larger vocabulary and varied sentence structure.
The YELLOW LEVEL presents more challenging ideas, a broad vocabulary, and wide variety in sentence structure.

When sharing a book with your child, read in short stretches, pausing often to talk about the pictures. Have your child turn the pages and point to the pictures and familiar words. And be sure to reread favorite stories or parts of stories.

There is no right or wrong way to share books with children. Find time to read with your child, and pass on the legacy of literacy.

Adria F. Klein, Ph.D.
Professor Emeritus
California State University
San Bernardino, California

First American edition published in 2003 by
Picture Window Books
5115 Excelsior Boulevard
Suite 232
Minneapolis, MN 55416
1-877-845-8392
www.picturewindowbooks.com

First published in Great Britain by Franklin Watts, 96 Leonard Street, London, EC2A 4XD
Text © Maeve Friel 2000
Illustration © Beccy Blake 2000

Printed in the United States of America.

Library of Congress Cataloging-in-Publication Data
Friel, Maeve.
  Felix on the move / written by Maeve Friel ; illustrated by Beccy Blake.—1st American ed.
   p. cm. — (Read-it! readers)
  Summary: Felix the cat is unhappy when movers take away everything down to his yellow
plastic bowl, but it all comes back along with his family.
  ISBN 1-4048-0055-7
  [1. Cats—Fiction. 2. Moving, Household—Fiction.] I. Blake, Beccy, ill. II. Title. III. Series.
PZ7.F91522 Fe 2003
  [E]—dc21   2002074803

Read-it! Readers
Red Level

Felix
on the Move

Written by Maeve Friel

Illustrated by Beccy Blake

Reading Advisors:
Adria F. Klein, Ph.D.
Professor Emeritus, California State University
San Bernardino, California

Ruth Thomas
Durham Public Schools
Durham, North Carolina

R. Ernice Bookout
Durham Public Schools
Durham, North Carolina

Picture Window Books
Minneapolis, Minnesota

Felix was a very happy cat.

He liked sitting on the windowsill

and napping in secret places.

He liked playing in the yard.

And he liked his family
so much, he gave them a
present every day.

One morning, a big van came to the house.

GOODE Movers

Out went the sofa where Felix liked to have his afternoon naps.

13

Out went the rug that he sharpened his claws on.

Out went the beds, the TV, and the refrigerator.

Worst of all, out went his
yellow plastic bowl.

Felix was not a happy cat.

Soon, there was nothing left but a cat basket.

"I'm not getting in that," growled Felix.

But he did!

Felix was all alone in an empty room.

25

Then in came the sofa, the rug, the TV, and the refrigerator.

In came his yellow plastic bowl.

Best of all, in came the family.

Felix settled down for a nap.

"This is the life," he purred.

"Home again!"

Red Level

The Best Snowman, by Margaret Nash 1-4048-0048-4
Bill's Baggy Pants, by Susan Gates 1-4048-0050-6
Cleo and Leo, by Anne Cassidy 1-4048-0049-2
Felix on the Move, by Maeve Friel 1-4048-0055-7
Jasper and Jess, by Anne Cassidy 1-4048-0061-1
The Lazy Scarecrow, by Jillian Powell 1-4048-0062-X
Little Joe's Big Race, by Andy Blackford 1-4048-0063-8
The Little Star, by Deborah Nash 1-4048-0065-4
The Naughty Puppy, by Jillian Powell 1-4048-0067-0
Selfish Sophie, by Damian Kelleher 1-4048-0069-7

Blue Level

The Bossy Rooster, by Margaret Nash 1-4048-0051-4
Jack's Party, by Ann Bryant 1-4048-0060-3
Little Red Riding Hood, by Maggie Moore 1-4048-0064-6
Recycled!, by Jillian Powell 1-4048-0068-9
The Sassy Monkey, by Anne Cassidy 1-4048-0058-1
The Three Little Pigs, by Maggie Moore 1-4048-0071-9

Yellow Level

Cinderella, by Barrie Wade 1-4048-0052-2
The Crying Princess, by Anne Cassidy 1-4048-0053-0
Eight Enormous Elephants, by Penny Dolan 1-4048-0054-9
Freddie's Fears, by Hilary Robinson 1-4048-0056-5
Goldilocks and the Three Bears, by Barrie Wade 1-4048-0057-3
Mary and the Fairy, by Penny Dolan 1-4048-0066-2
Jack and the Beanstalk, by Maggie Moore 1-4048-0059-X
The Three Billy Goats Gruff, by Barrie Wade 1-4048-0070-0